Hattie Mae's Halloween

by Claudine C. Wargel

Illustrations by Joseph Mugisha

Cover Art by Marjorie A. Kauth

ISBN: 978-0-692-75888-5

This book is dedicated to:
My folks, who put up with my hayloft shenanigans;
Mrs. Corgan, who helped me discover my love of writing;
June Snell, who was an inspiration;
and my husband, who is plain amazing.

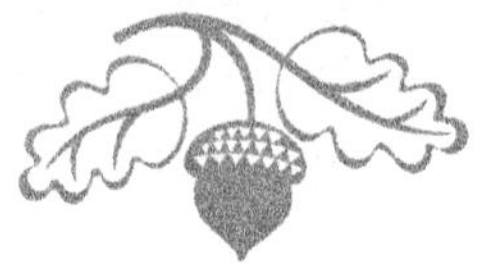

CONTENTS

MISS HATTIE MAE BRAMBLE

Hattie Mae Bramble was an ordinary girl. She was a bit taller, but not much prettier, than most of the girls in her 5th grade class. Her grades were good, but not the very best. She wasn't a bookworm, or a jock, a chorus girl or a wallflower. Hattie Mae was just, well, Hattie Mae.

Hattie Mae's hair was "the color of autumn leaves," her mother liked to say. Except, that is, the two gray strands that sprung from the crown of her head. They had been there as long as Hattie and her mother could remember.

"Those two just didn't get colored," the hair stylist explained again and again. But Hattie and her mom could never be certain.

Perhaps it was made up for by Hattie's eyes, which were the swirling blue of a treasured marble. Mrs. Brimwood, Hattie's homeroom teacher, said those eyes "glitter with imagination," and Mrs. Brimwood was pretty much always right.

Mrs. Brimwood was kind and roundish to look at. She loved, loved, loved to tell stories and read poems. That was her thing. Mrs. Pinchly taught math, and that was her thing. Mrs. Brimwood gave

Hattie Mae good grades, but—you know--not the very best. Hattie listened in class and tried hard. Truth be told, she fancied herself to be smart, and figured others didn't know it just yet. She always kept that notion to herself—like she was holding something special in a hidden pocket.

If you asked Hattie Mae's brothers (and she has two), they might say something different.

"Sis? Yeah, she thinks she's mysterious or something. She's mysterious, all right! Why would anyone put a cat on the bathroom scales? Or ask the librarian about turtle food?" big brother Finn would say.

Well, Hattie would keep THAT to herself, at least for now. What Hattie Mae knew was she hoped to be a veterinarian one day. She was practicing right now, you might say. The farm where she and her family lived was the perfect place—full of animals, from small and sweet to large and smelly.

It was Hattie's job to look after the "small animals" as her Dad often called them. That was a veterinary term, he told her. Hattie fed the cats and gave water to Babe, the stray dog the family had grown to love.

There was one thing Hattie loved almost as much as she loved her animals, and that was dressing up. Which may be why Halloween was Hattie's very favorite holiday. And is probably why Hattie was utterly, wonderfully and completely excited about the Halloween celebration at her school this very year.

2

HALLOWEEN AHEAD

"Children, children…I need your attention," Mrs. Brimwood said in a full-bodied voice. Her pink face was filled with a huge smile. "Next week is the annual Cottonwood Community Grade School costume parade!"

Everyone knew the parade was coming, still Hattie and her classmates squealed with delight.

"The Costume Parade!" sighed Charlot Reynolds, her face aglow with pleasure.

"Woooee!" said Sadie Range, nearly shivering with excitement.

"Class, listen," said Mrs. Brimwood. "As usual, Principal Greenlow will give out one prize for each grade level. Most of all, he wants everyone to be creative!"

"What are the prizes? What are the prizes?" yelped Junior Overby.

"Well, as you know, they are always quite special," said Mrs. Brimwood. "This year, it's going to be a surprise. But I KNOW you're going to love it!"

The children were stumped. It was so hard to wait. They sat pondering and soon began guessing.

"A pizza party for the winner's classroom?"

home work

asked Charlot.

"I bet it's a frog for the boys or a hamster if it's a girl," smirked Toby Ebersol.

"And then, what if the hamster ate the frog!" said Zeke Rule, who sat next to Toby.

"Yeah...," Toby began, but Mrs. Brimwood interrupted.

"That's enough, class," she said in her best "I mean business" voice.

Hattie Mae wasn't in trouble. She hadn't guessed at the prize. She hadn't spoken up at all. She was too busy thinking. After all, she was kind of smart. Already she was planning her way to the stage where costume awards would be handed out in two short weeks.

3

SCHOOL'S OUT

With that, the school day was over. The bell rang, and Hattie Mae and Charlot raced for the door. It was their favorite day of the week, Tuesday. Soon, Charlot's mother appeared. The girls hopped into her dusty white van, and they zoomed across town to the Cottonwood Brethren Church.

"What do you think?" Hattie Mae asked Charlot. "What are you going to be for Halloween this year?"

"Not sure," said Charlot. "Still working on it."

"Yeah, me too," said Hattie Mae.

"Oh, come on, Hattie. You can never resist being a witch. You've been a witch every year I can remember! And that's a lot of years!" Charlot laughed.

"Hey, you never know," said Hattie Mae. "This is fifth grade. This is different!"

"So true," said Charlot with a shrug.

They were growing up, at least a little. Only the sixth graders were bigger in their school. Hattie and Charlot knew more things and more people than they ever had before. And they were very full of ideas.

"You know, Miss Conley will probably help

Cindy Cunningham again," Charlot groaned.

Cindy was Miss Conley's niece, and Miss Conley taught sewing and cooking at Cottonwood Junior High. And from Miss Conley, Cindy took as much help as she could possibly get.

"It's so unfair," said Charlot.

"Yeah, but this year could be different," said Hattie. "You just never really know."

4

"TUESDAY TIME"

More of the girls' friends were waiting at the church, buzzing about who would dress as what for the school Halloween contest. Lynn and Marissa were there. So were Junior and Toby from school. It was a fun group.

June White ran Tuesday Time, filling it with silly songs, games and rounding up the moms to cook great meals.

Soon, Hattie and her friends filled the church

choir loft and belted out tunes as June directed with big waves of her arm. As June sang along, she moved her mouth more than was needed and raised her eyebrows sky-high.

"GLO-OOO—RY!" she exclaimed, showing how the song, "Oh, Great God of Glory" was supposed to end.

It reminded Hattie of the time she stayed with Toby's family. Her folks were out of town. Toby had three brothers, and it was as if they had never seen a girl. Those brothers watched Hattie like she was some kind of freak. The two littlest ones followed her everywhere, their round faces staring up at her. No matter. The funniest thing was their church, or really, their choir director. He sang every word a good measure before his choir! Shouting it.

"ANGELS…!!" he blared, only to be followed seconds later by the church group. He never seemed to notice, but Hattie sure did.

"….MOUNTAIN HIGH!" he honked again.

And again and again. At one service, Hattie and Toby had been overcome by giggles. Sitting near the church's front, they tried to stop. The more they tried, the more they giggled. By the end, they nearly peed their pants. Truly. It wasn't pretty.

Well, June may have looked silly, but she was pretty normal compared to Toby's choir director--and loads of fun. Soon, Marissa's mom was doling out huge piles of steaming spaghetti. Hattie filed past and sat down with Charlot.

"Okay, guys," said June. She always called them

guys—not children or kids or girls and boys. "It's been a great night. I know you're already thinking about Halloween, but don't forget my special program this weekend. I'll be here with the Pleasant Hill Porkettes, and you don't want to miss it! You might even find some Halloween inspiration."

"Pleasant Hill Porkettes?" I turned to Charlot in wonderment.

"I have no idea," said Charlot. "I really don't."

Whatever the case, Hattie was sure June was right—she didn't want to miss it.

5

THE NEW BABIES

At home that night, Hattie was doodling costume ideas—witches on brooms mostly--in a notebook when her father pulled her aside.

"There's something I'd like you to see," he said secretively. "Come outside with me."

Hattie and her dad bundled up. She put on her chore coat—the one she used when she was going to the barn or feeding the cats and the dog. She pulled on her mud boots. They were army green with heavy soles. They stepped outside into the crisp, cool October night.

Across the large, circle driveway lay the barns. The one for the cattle had hay stored above. That place was called the hayloft. Standing on one side of that barn were two tall, dark blue silos, which held chopped corn plants called silage.

Hattie and her dad headed for a second barn. It was white washed with flat pieces of wood layered for a roof. The barn towered above, but they entered a dark door under a big, lower roof, passing tractors and wagons as they walked. In the back of the barn were several rooms where the hogs lived.

Hattie and her dad stepped into the building, moving quietly.

"Sshhh," he mouthed to her.

They moved silently in the dark barn toward the back where an orange glow could be seen. There, under a heat lamp lie Esmerelda. The large pinkish-white pig lay very still, her stomach rising and falling with gentle breathing. Soft, happy grunting sounds came one after another from her throat.

"Oh, my!" Hattie exclaimed, her face beaming at her father.

Esmerelda had babies! There were ten. They huddled one on top of another, drinking milk from her udder. There was a place for each one. And there they lay, wiggling and nursing and pushing their tiny hooves into their mother's udder.

"Amazing, isn't it?" asked Hattie's dad.

"Yes. Amazing," said Hattie, ever so glad she had left her costume doodling to come outside.

6

THE PLEASANT HILL PORKETTES

One pig, two pigs, three pigs, four… Four pigs danced across the floor of the Cottonwood Community Church fellowship hall. Well, they were pigs—sort of. Hattie sat with her friends and all their parents watching June White's Porkettes. Everyone roared with laughter. Whatever the creatures were, they were hysterical!

One of the critters wore blue-jean bib overalls. Three wore red and white checkered dresses with flouncy, swirly skirts trimmed in rickrack and lace. The costumes were so creative! Plastic bottles with painted faces were a great disguise. The boy pig wore a straw hat on top, and the girls wore red-haired wigs. The boy wore boots. The girls wore high heels. And leading down the front of each belly were rows of lady's bras!

Hattie pointed and leaned over to Charlot. "That's the udder," she said. "That's where the baby pigs get their milk!"

"Oh!" giggled Charlot. "That's silly!"

The redheaded pigs moved to the front, dancing in rhythm with the country music. They began to high kick, standing side-by-side with their arms and shoulders together, locking the pigs into one long row.

There was more laughter. Roaring laughter.

"Unmask yourself you masked pigs!" Charlot's dad yelled over the music.

Instead, the beat of the music quickened, and the pigs began to move in a whole new way. The lead girl pig moved forward, stepping, twisting and pumping a fist in the air.

"Unmask yourselves!" yelled Evan Lock, a young man who farmed near Hattie's place.

Hattie and Charlot chimed in, and soon the group was chanting at the pigs to show their faces. Suddenly, the music ended. The pigs stopped in their spots and flung off their wigs and masks.

Now everyone knew. The lead pig was none other than June White.

"Thanks for watching," said June, still catching her breath from her dance. "These are my friends, the Porkettes! We're here to remind you to make wholesome, yummy pork a part of your meals."

June lived on a farm, too, Hattie remembered. Now things were making sense.

"Are you kidding?" said Mr. Lock. "Nothing beats a pork chop!"

"Hmphhh," grumbled someone in the back. It was Clarissa Wheeler, who at age 16 had declared herself a vegan.

But June didn't care, and neither did anyone else. The crowd jumped to their feet, giggling and clapping for the best band of dancing pigs they had ever seen.

Yes, now Hattie could truly see it. She could see why June had said she shouldn't miss this show. And she could definitely see why June said it might hold some "Halloween inspiration."

7

AN IDEA IS BORN

"More, please," said Charlot.

It was chicken fried steak day at the cafeteria. It was not Hattie's favorite, but she was starving after a long morning of studies. Who knew books and numbers could make you so hungry?

Hattie and Charlot wolfed down their meals, finding time to squeeze in a few words between each bite.

"You gotta costume idea yet?" asked Sadie

Range, who sat with them.

"Naw," said Charlot. "I'm workin' on something special. You know, original."

"I'm thinking of going as a leprechaun, but don't tell anyone," said Sadie.

"Oooh, that's good. Can you do that for Halloween?" asked Hattie.

"Sure," said Sadie. "Anything goes."

Their food now gone, they ran for the asphalt pavement that served as the floor for the Cottonwood Community Grade School playground.

They quickly laid claim to the monkey bars near a tree. There, Charlot and Hattie perched like the robins and blackbirds, watching their classmates for a moment. Cindy, Sara and Denise played soccer. Toby and Zeke spun the merry-go-round, making Maci squeal with gleeful dizziness.

Hattie hopped down from the monkey bars.

"Come on," she chirped to Charlot.

On the ground, Hattie grabbed Charlot and spun her to face her. Eyes wide and cheeks bunched up, Hattie shown a bright grin at her friend.

"What? What!" asked Charlot. "What are you thinking now? You're scaring me a little!"

"I've got it!" Hattie exclaimed. "I know what I'm going to be for Halloween!"

"Oh!" giggled Charlot, who was a little relieved.

"And, I know what YOU are going to be for Halloween, too!"

"Oh!" said Charlot, eyeing her friend. She was no longer relieved.

8

MOTHER, DEAR...

Hattie rushed through the front door and tossed down her book bag. It was just 10 days until the school costume contest, and time for Hattie to let her mother know about her costume secret.

"Momma!" Hattie yelled.

"Momma!" she yelled again, her excitement getting the better of her.

"Just a minute, dear," answered Rae Ann Bramble, her voice muffled by the coats hanging in a closet she seemed to be cleaning. She was forever cleaning. Or sewing or gardening or helping Hattie's dad with the farming.

Hattie's mother rustled her way out of the closet, freeing herself from a red scarf clinging to her head. She tossed it aside in a rush, then stood staring intensely at Hattie.

"All right. Now. Whatever is so urgent?" she asked her daughter with a small sigh.

"Well," said Hattie, "there's this costume contest at school…"

"Yes," said her mother.

"…and I've got the greatest idea…"

"Yes," said her mother.

"...I know we can win the contest, and even if we don't it'll still be so cool!"

"Uh, huh," said Hattie's mother, crinkling her eyes and pursing her lips as she studied her only daughter.

"Yeah, definitely! No one else is going to think of it," Hattie said.

"And let me guess. You're going to need a bit of my help?" asked Hattie's mother, which was less a question than a statement.

"Yes, oh, yes," said Hattie Mae. "We're going to need your help."

About that time, Charlot tumbled into the room.

"Wow, in a hurry much?" Hattie asked. Charlot was catching her breath. She had just arrived from her home across the road.

"I ran over as soon as I saw you were home…" Charlot's voice slowly faded as her eyes darted around the yellowish room. Small baskets lined shelves on the walls. One brimmed with dried seedpods. Another held gourds. A set of shelves was stacked with neatly folded fabric of every color. There were piles of ancient looking doorknobs, and crocks filled with birch tree sticks. Charlot's eye caught a frame on the wall.

"Rae Ann Bramble, Master Preserver, University of Illinois Cooperative Extension," read the yellowed paper inside the frame.

Through a door Charlot could see the kitchen,

its counters covered with tomatoes and zucchini. Further on in a breezeway, crates for catching fish were stacked near lawn chairs.

Charlot's eyes were wide with wonder. Her house was nothing like this. Neither was her mother. But luckily for both Charlot and Hattie, Hattie's mother was a keeper of useful things.

Hattie's mother was prepared when October rolled around each year. She had set aside lace and old hats, black fabric, shells, beads and old spectacles. Soon, Hattie and Charlot spilled their Halloween idea. Even Hattie's mother was a bit surprised that Hattie and Charlot wanted nothing more than to dress up for Halloween…as pigs.

BUILDING THE COSTUME

Before Hattie could bat an eye, her mother was digging in the yellow room behind the antique pine door. There, in cabinets her grandfather had built, were stacks and drawers and boxes of sewing and craft supplies.

The room was the color of corn, and it was there that Hattie's mother saved nearly everything. She had seen years with little rain, years with little growing in the field to harvest and sell, especially when she had been a young child on the farm. Although she now had everything she needed and more, Hattie's mother remembered days of having little. So she saved things, just in case.

Hattie brushed past the clothing rack lined with her father's work shirts. Later she would iron them for five cents each. They were all cotton to keep him cool, but they wrinkled badly. Did Daddy really need his shirts ironed to ride on a tractor? Hattie wasn't sure, but her mom and dad thought so, and it meant money for her!

Hattie's mother pulled open the dark walnut doors of a large cabinet. Inside were stacks of cotton fabric in many colors, waiting to be sewn into shirts for Hattie's father. Hattie's mother pushed the fabric aside, reached to the back and pulled out a large piece of gingham—red and white checked, with white stars in the middle of the red squares.

"Perfect!" exclaimed Hattie's mother.

"Oh, my. Yes!" Hattie agreed.

"Hattie, go dig through the boxes on the second shelf behind the ironing board," her mother said.

"Okay, ma," said Hattie.

Inside one box were castoff silk flowers. Hattie picked through, selecting tiny bunches of red, white and blue flowers.

"Here, ma. These would look great on a straw hat, for the girl pig," said Hattie.

In the bathroom closet, Rae Ann stored a few extra clothes. They came in handy when cousins or friends stopped by and, somehow, ended up covered in mud or snow. In the closet Hattie found a pair of old denim bibs. With a leather belt on top, they'd fit Charlot just fine. White plastic bleach jugs were nice and pointy, and would make a fine hog snout.

And so it went until most of the supplies were gathered. Hattie was feeling very satisfied, but the costume was not yet complete. Something like a pig herself, Hattie's mother was rooting in a dark corner of the laundry room. She pulled out a large, worn out straw hat for Charlot's boy pig. Jostling aside old iron-on mending patches, she pulled out one final treasure--old bra cups, salvaged from bras that were long worn out. Why on earth her mother had kept those, Hattie would never know. But at this moment, Hattie was certainly glad that her mother was the mother of all packrats.

10

A LITTLE NUDGE

"Five days," said Charlot.

"Five days," said Hattie, answering her friend with a serious face.

The two then broke out in giggles.

"No one else will think of it," said Charlot, a little smug.

"Yeah, there's no way," said Hattie.

It was early evening and the two were strolling across Hattie's circle drive toward the whitewashed barns to check on Esmeralda. They stepped into the dark, moist air of the barn.

"Eeeew!" said Charlot.

"Oh, Charlot! Buck up! It's just a little hog poo. It's not so bad," Hattie exclaimed.

"Hmmm. Not so sure about that, my friend," Charlot answered.

They walked down the cool, musty hall in the darkness toward the spot where the yellow lamp was glowing.

"Sshhh," said Hattie.

Charlot looked at her with a question mark written across her face.

"Wha?" she said quietly.

"SShhhh!" said Hattie again, leaning toward her friend with big eyes to make her point.

Charlot shrugged and stepped in line behind Hattie, placing each foot softly on the concrete floor. They crept along silently until they emerged near a wooden gate. Yellow light shone between the slats. Crouching there they peered between the gate boards. Esmeralda lay nursing her piglets.

"Oh-my-gosh!" screeched Charlot in the tiniest squeal she could manage. "That's amazing! The babies are adorable. And I SO understand the costume now!"

Hattie was sure Esmeralda had not heard them, but the lumbering sow began to get up. She really was huge, many times the size of her tiny babies.

Esmeralda began to push her weight upward, shaking free of the many piglets that lay next to her. She stood, grunting above the babies. Most of the piglets stood on wobbly legs and began to scatter, but one continued to lie in the warm straw, happily snoozing with its belly full of milk. Esmeralda lowered her massive head, giving the piglet a gentle nudge with her snout. The baby awoke with a squeal, skittering across the pig pen in a streak.

Hattie and Charlot giggled.

"You sure don't get to see something like this every day!" said Charlot.

"You sure don't," thought Hattie to herself. Some folks would never see something like that at all, as long as they lived. For a moment, she just stood and thought of it—of how lucky she was to live on a farm. She was lucky to have the animals. And lucky to have the ideas they gave her.

11

COSTUME UP

Then one Friday in late October, Hattie awoke with a start. Today was the day! The sun shone and a brisk breeze blew. Hattie could hear her father, already starting equipment and preparing to head to the field. He had started to harvest the corn many weeks ago, and was nearly finished. In the Bramble family, the start of harvest always marked the beginning of fall. But for Hattie, fall could never, NEVER be complete without Halloween.

"Omigosh, Mom! The costume parade is today!" Hattie nearly screeched the words.

She tried to calm herself, bringing her voice down about an octave. In a low, almost whispering voice she began again…

"I talked to Charlot last night. She's all set. Her bibs fit, and her jug face is made. I gave her that corn-cob pipe, and she has a basket of plastic eggs to carry. I know hogs don't gather eggs, of course, it's just the farm theme, you know…"

Hattie's mother nodded her head, but kept her eyes on her pancake batter. It was never good to multi-task when cooking, she always said. She added mix. Stir. Pour. Flip. Stack. Quickly a tower of steaming pancakes grew.

Excitement continued to stream from Hattie's mouth as her little brother Dirk wandered from the back of the house, rubbing sleep from his eyes.

"Mornin'," he said.

"G'morning!" Hattie chirped.

Dirk, still in his pajamas, dragged orange and blue clothing items behind him, as well as a football helmet bearing a fancy-faced Indian chief. He slumped at the kitchen table, chugging down a tiny glass of orange juice in one slurp.

"It's game day," he said, puffing out his chest and grinning big.

"Hmm," said Hattie. "Are you pretending University of Illinois player again?"

"Beats acting like farm animals…" Dirk began.

"At least mine's based in reality!" Hattie quipped.

"Now, children..." Hattie's mother interrupted, finally looking up from the pancakes. "Do you have to start this so early?"

Dirk wasn't listening. Neither was Hattie.

"When's the last time Esmeralda wore a skirt?" sneered Dirk.

"Children...how about for Halloween, you pretend to get along?" their mother said in a sugary voice. "Hattie, let's focus now. Is your homework done?"

"Uhh..." Hattie pulled her gaze from her brother's squinting eyes, trying to refocus.

"Check," said Hattie.

"Piano books packed?"

"Check," said Hattie.

"Kids, is your lunch money packed?"

"Check," they both said together.

Hattie and Dirk caught the bus that morning. That wasn't always the case. The bus seemed littered with extra bags. Everyone had their costume in tow. No one was talking, though, and that included Hattie.

Cindy was first to speak. Hattie had caught Cindy looking at the plastic trash bag she was toting. The bag was lumpy, and a triangle shape poked out one side.

"It's a witch!" said Cindy very matter-of-fact. "You're a witch again. I knew it! Did you miss that bulletin about being original?"

Hattie chuckled to herself but made no reply. That was hard, but she did it. She "held her tongue," as June always called it.

"What are you this year?" asked Hattie, changing the subject and sounding almost polite.

"I'm not saying," quipped Cindy. And that was that.

At school the day passed more slowly than ever, it seemed to Hattie. She did what she could to pass the time. When she'd completed her work she doodled kitten faces on her notebook. Lunchtime passed. English passed and then science and then finally, finally it was time.

One by one the children went off to the restroom or to the coat closet, which was like a big, dark tunnel with doors on each end. Each emerged in a costume. Some you could barely recognize.

Sadie emerged as a leprechaun, just as she had promised. Toby had been transformed into a giant M & M. It figured. He always had food on his mind! Zeke had transformed into, well, a Transformer, in fact. Naturally, every year there was at least one princess. This year it was Cindy, dressed as Cinderella. The approach was a bit original, though, Hattie noted.

"Back when mom was in school, she wore this dress to her prom," said Cindy.

It was pink satin with layers of lace over the top. At the bottom edge, one layer of shimmery pink draped like a row of fluffy curtains. Yep, that would have been perfect "back in the day," thought Hattie.

"She made it for her 4-H project that year," Cindy continued. "Went to state, she did."

Now, Hattie was impressed.

"You're kidding," Hattie exclaimed. "Do you think she'd make a dress for me? Well, okay, maybe not a dress…"

"Hattie Mae Bramble!" called Mrs. Brimwood "It's your turn in the changing room."

"Charlot's gotta go, too, Mrs. Brimwood," said Hattie.

"Right. Charlot Reynolds!" cried Mrs. Brimwood.

Hattie headed for the coat closet with her bag in hand. Charlot followed close behind.

They stepped into their outfits. Hattie reached into her garbage bag, grabbing the pointy thing that Cindy had seen. They strapped on their bleach bottle pig snouts and added the accessories. A bandana here, a corn cob pipe there. Soon, they were fully outfitted and walked out into the room.

Alone, they were interesting, thought Charlot. But together, they were amazing. Hattie was equally pleased. One thing was certain: no one could say that Hattie and Charlot weren't original.

12

HATTIE'S SURPRISE

As they stepped out onto the hardwood plank floor of the classroom to face Mrs. Brimwood, a flicker of surprise crossed the teacher's face. Soon, she darted from the room, disappearing down the hall.

Before long, Mrs. Pinchly appeared. Her face looked strained and flushed.

"Hattie Bramble?" she said softly. "Hattie, please come with me."

"Oh. Okay," said Hattie. Feeling a bit uncertain, she turned and smiled at Charlot anyway. "See you in a bit!"

"Okay," said Charlot.

Hattie followed Mrs. Pinchly down the hall. Soon, the teacher spun on her heel, opening the door to the speech room. That was where kids went to learn to say sounds the right way. Mrs. Pinchly stepped inside and motioned to Hattie to do the same. They were now quietly tucked inside the small room.

"Have a seat, dear," said Mrs. Pinchly, waving her hand toward a smallish table and an even smaller chair.

Mrs. Pinchly was a soft-spoken teacher and rarely became upset with anyone. But as she turned to Hattie, she seemed to bristle.

"Hattie..." she started. "Do you really intend to wear that costume today?"

At first, Hattie wasn't sure she had heard right.

"What?" she asked.

"Do you really intend to wear that costume today?" Mrs. Pinchly said again.

Yep, she had heard right. Hattie sat quietly for a moment. Her head felt like it was spinning a bit.

"Well, of course, I do," said Hattie, with some excitement—and some confusion in her voice. She was very surprised to be asked that question!

"Do you really think you'll be comfortable in that?" the teacher asked, putting extra emphasis on the word "comfortable."

"Sure," said Hattie quickly, still confused.

What was Mrs. Pinchly thinking, she wondered? Why on earth wouldn't Hattie want to wear the costume? She had certainly worked on it very hard!

Mrs. Pinchly was staring down at her own hands, studying her perfectly-painted fingernails it seemed. They were a dull, boring color that was probably called "buff" or "nude," Hattie thought. Mrs. Pinchly flattened one hand, held it out and peered at it. Still, she had more questions for Hattie.

"Does your mother know you're wearing that?" Mrs. Pinchly asked, pointing at Hattie's costume with her buff-tipped finger.

"Well, sure. Of course, she does!" Hattie said. "She helped me make it!"

Mrs. Pinchly stared straight at Hattie now. Her face had gone white and she was blinking like a twinkle light on its way to burning out.

Hattie felt her own face begin to burn hotly. Her eyes stung, and a lump had formed in her throat. She wouldn't cry, she thought to herself. There was no reason to cry. But she was so confused! Of course her mother knew, she thought! Why was Mrs. Pinchly asking her all of these questions?

"Well, don't you think it's a bit...inappropriate?" she hesitated and gestured at Hattie's abdomen, which was covered with rows of old bras furnished by Hattie's mom. "...Isn't it just really inappropriate?"

Hattie paused, then said slowly, "Gosh, no, I don't think so! I mean, my mother did help make it!"

Mrs. Pinchly looked at Hattie blankly. She blinked a good bit more.

Hattie felt lonely, like the world was big and she was small. Her chest felt heavy, and the lump was stuck in her throat. She was definitely confused, but one thing was clear. Mrs. Pinchly did not like her costume.

Since all was quiet for a moment, Hattie decided to mount an argument. Maybe Mrs. Pinchly just didn't know how mother pigs are made. That was probably the issue, she decided.

"Okay, if it's the bras you're worried about, the costume really needs them. You see, this is the mother pig's udder. It's how the baby pigs are fed. I know. We have some hogs, and I have one named Esmerelda. She's a great mom…"

"Well, yes, Hattie. I do know that," said Mrs. Pinchly, rolling her eyes a bit. Then, she went silent again.

Hattie took a moment to think. Mother does think the costume is fine, she thought to herself. And June White had worn it to dance. And the dancing had been done at her church, for crying out loud! This simply had to be okay, Hattie decided.

"You know, my costume goes with Charlot's," said Hattie, finally. "I really have to wear it. Without my costume, Charlot's costume won't make any sense."

"So, that's your decision?" asked Mrs. Pinchly, putting a sharp point on her question. "You're going to wear it?"

"Yes. I am," said Hattie, solidly, as if there had never been any question about it.

"Well, I can't stop you, but I think it's a mistake," said Mrs. Pinchly. "I can tell you that, if I were you, I would not wear that."

Yes, Hattie was certain of that. Mrs. Pinchly wouldn't wear it. But Hattie would. She would not let down her friend.

Hattie did her best to smile politely. Somehow she knew that, in her own way, Mrs. Pinchly was surely trying to help. She was a teacher, after all.

"Hmphh. Very irreverent," said Mrs. Pinchly, pursing her mouth and giving Hattie one last disappointed shake of the head. Then, she showed Hattie the speech room door.

Hattie walked out and back to her classroom,

following Mrs. Pinchly. The teacher pulled aside Hattie's homeroom teacher, Mrs. Brimwood, for a moment. Mrs. Brimwood's eyes darted to Hattie, and she knew she was the topic of their talk.

Wow, thought Hattie. Did Mrs. Brimwood think the costume was a bad idea, too? Had she asked Mrs. Pinchly to take Hattie to the speech room? Despite her decision, Hattie felt uncertain. Her eyes were stinging and that lump was stuck in her throat. She was sure she wanted to wear the costume, but she was not at all sure what would happen next. Would anyone judging the costume contest even understand this pair of pigs?

Would Hattie's own mother and June White lead her to do something inappropriate? She didn't think so…but Hattie was about to find out for sure.

13

GET READY

Hattie had never seen the gymnasium so full. Parents were packed shoulder to shoulder, filling the creaky wooden bleachers. A few babies cried and squirmed. Bright sunshine shown through foggy window panes above the bleachers, as the odd father coughed here and there. But mostly, mothers whispered to one another, smiled and pointed to their children.

Hattie's dad was in the field, and her mom was teaching a class on canning foods at the local hardware store. That was okay. This was Hattie's thing. And she was in the 5th grade, after all. She didn't need her hand held.

Charlot stood next to Hattie in the hallway near the stage no one ever used. Second graders were parading across the gym. It would be time for Hattie's class before long. The fourth graders assembled into a long line across the gym, fidgeting and waving to their parents.

Mrs. Pith, a fourth grade teacher, seemed to be in charge. Her coal-black hair was tall on top and flipped out at her neck. It bounced like it was one piece when she shook her head for emphasis, which was actually quite often. She held the microphone and a piece of paper that had been handed to her by the judges.

Mrs. Pith glanced down the row of children, looked at her paper, and then called a little boy forward. The parents erupted in applause, smiling at one another in approval. The winning child beamed as Mrs. Pith pressed something small and shiny into his hand.

Hattie's classmates craned their necks.

"What is it?" asked Robbie.

"I saw something shiny," said Toby.

"Our turn children," said Mrs. Brimwood, calling the group out into the gymnasium.

Charlot turned to Hattie, grabbed her hand and

squeezed it, then smiled brightly into her friend's face.

"Good luck!" said Charlot to Hattie.

"Good luck!" said Hattie to Charlot.

Together, they took a deep breath, tightened their handhold and walked out into the gymnasium.

14

HOG WILD

Soon there were "oohs" and "aaawes" and pointing. The children paraded in front of the crowd, some pausing or turning briefly for the parents. Marissa, dressed as a ballerina, threw in a twirl for good measure.

"Arrg. That dance class!" her twin brother, who was dressed as Yoda, mumbled under his breath, walking a step behind her in alphabetical order.

There was no second place. No runner up, merit award or consolation prize. You won or you didn't. Hattie knew it was just a costume contest. Her mother had told her that winning wasn't always important. But, of course, she did want to win. What was it about winning that felt so good? Hattie wasn't sure, but she wanted to know.

Now in front of the parents, in the middle of the gym, Hattie and Charlot looked at one another. They grinned, nodded, then linked arms and did a square-dance turn on the shiny wooden floor. The parents noticed, and answered with loud clapping. A shiver went down Hattie's back, and she stood a bit taller. Then, the two turned, and waited with their class, happy that Halloween had finally come.

Now Mrs. Brimwood was stepping into the middle of the gym. She took a paper from the table

of judges, who sat with their lips tight, like a group of students who had just been scolded. Mrs. Brimwood walked and walked. It was taking her forever, thought Hattie, as she watched Mrs. Brimwood's slow-moving legs. What was she waiting for?

"I want to congratulate my entire class," she finally said into the microphone. The microphone made a loud squawking noise.

"Oops. Sorry," she said, when the racket ended. "All right, then. We asked the children to be original this year. I think they listened, don't you?"

Again, the parents began to clap loudly.

"We couldn't choose just one winner," she went on, "and you'll see why. Hattie Mae Bramble and Charlot Reynolds, you are our winners! I think they were original, don't you?"

Now the gym erupted into loud clapping. The loudest dad, who turned out to be Charlot's father, gave a happy hoot. Hattie and Charlot walked up, beaming at Mrs. Brimwood. For each, Mrs. Brimwood pressed a warm and very shiny large silver coin into the palm of her hand. It was a collectible Presidential Dollar Coin.

Hattie looked up into her teacher's face. Mrs. Brimwood grinned and winked at Hattie, and the girl wondered why she had ever doubted the best teacher she ever had.

Hattie knew it wasn't right to say, "I told you so." She would never do that to Mrs. Pinchly, of course. But she probably didn't have to. The teacher was nestled with her own class at the back of the gym. As the parents roared with applause and Mr. Reynolds hollered, Mrs. Pinchly's face shown as red as the brightest valentine. Well, thought Hattie, maybe that was okay. Maybe even teachers could sometimes learn something. Like girl pigs should have udders. Maybe today, Mrs. Pinchly would figure out that originality really was all right sometimes, even if it made a few people uncomfortable.

15

THE LAST WORD

After school, Hattie's mother was anxious to learn about her daughter's day—all the interesting costumes, the little jig Hattie and Charlot had done, and even about Mrs. Pinchly's odd reaction.

"Really?" Hattie's mother had asked, again and again, as Hattie told her about the trip to the speech room.

"Yeah, really!" said Hattie, her eyes huge.

Hattie checked her cats, fed the turtle, and asked Rae Ann if Charlot could spend the night, just to celebrate.

"You bet," said Hattie's mom.

After dinner, the girls did Hattie's evening chores. Putting away a few toys, they headed to the barn to give Esmeralda clean water, fresh straw for bedding, and a big scoop of ground corn. "Come here, Charlot," said Hattie.

"Hmm?" said her best friend. "Okay."

Hattie knelt down near the big sow's pen, looking between the boards of the wooden gate, into the warm glow of the heat lamp where the baby pigs lay sleeping in a steamy pile.

Esmeralda lumbered over to the fence, staring at the girls.

"Essy, we won!" Hattie whispered to the pig.

The pig gave a soft, motherly grunt and, Hattie was sure, her pink mouth curved into one truly special smile.

- The End -

Don't miss Hattie's next adventure!

1

MR. PINCHLY

A bold October sun shone down on top of my head, warming my auburn hair. I was walking. Well gliding, really. I glided among the rows and racks of ceramic pots. I floated past once-bright trays of flowers and herbs, now on their last legs.

Foompth! I stopped and the shadow behind me rammed into me from head to toe. The back of my left shoe went flat. The scrape of another shoe raked down the back of my heel.

"Dirk! Really?!" I winced and reached down to sooth the back of my foot.

Little brother Dirk and I were checking out the stock at Mr. Pinchly's garden shop. Dirk seemed forever bored and had insisted on tagging along with mom and me. That's what he did. He followed. Maybe one day, he would have an idea of his own.

"When Mom said you should stay close, I don't think I meant THAT close," I snapped at Dirk.

He was just ten and as I spoke to him, he shrank away, just a bit. At the budding age of twelve, I had grown. Dirk, not so much. I had become a rather willowy fifth grader, and stood a good head taller than Dirk. In fact, I was nearly the tallest girl in my class. But not quite.

I looked down at Dirk, squinting my eyes and pursing my lips as if I were angry. In my little brother's face I saw a pink flush from the afternoon sun, and a nose sprinkled with a few freckles. His almond-shaped eyes were warm brown, and he raised his eyebrows as I peered at him.

"What's up, Hattie?" he asked innocently, pretending he had no idea what he had done.

Yep, Hattie. Hattie Mae Bramble, actually. My parents gave me a name from the 1860s, even though I was born in the 1960s. That's how it felt, anyway. Hattie Mae had been my great aunt's name. My brothers, Dirk and Finn, somehow got normal names. I tried to embrace my name. Hattie was original, unique. So was I, I figured.

My foot was still stinging from the scuff. But my scowl dissolved into a smile as I grabbed my brother's arm.

"Come on," I said. "Let's go check out the gourds and stuff. Maybe Mom will let us buy some things to decorate for fall."

I did love fall, especially on the Central Illinois farm where we lived. I loved the crisp weather, the falling leaves and the rainbow of colors created by the trees. I loved to smell warm field corn pouring into my father's grain bins during harvest, and the scent of the chainsaw on his coat after he cut up a fallen tree. In the feedlot with my father on fall mornings, I could see the cattle breathe, each puff creating a little cloud in the gray morning mist.

Gliding again, I studied Mr. Pinchly's produce. The pumpkins, gourds and Indian corn would make a great fall porch display. And maybe add in a bale of hay. It was Saturday, and Mr. Pinchly's little garden shop was full of shoppers. His wife was Mrs. Pinchly, my math teacher, but on weekends she ran the cash register in the garden shop, ringing up sale after sale. Everyone in Cottonwood, it seemed, loved to decorate for fall.

Dirk walked beside me now, hoping to avoid another crash. That's how it often was, with Dirk following me through my day. He followed when I went to the pasture to feed our pony, Susie, and to feed the farm dog, Babe. He followed when I climbed into our treehouse--the one Finn had built with a little help from Dirk and me. He even followed me into the hayloft, which is where I went to be alone and listen to the quiet.

But really, who else was Dirk going to play with? Finn was now almost old enough to drive and didn't want to do little kid things. He was already allowed to drive a tractor on the farm. Many days after school and on weekends, Finn was busy helping Dad in the field. When he wasn't, he seemed only to find ways to pester me and Dirk. Sometimes he hid and pelted Dirk with pebbles. Other times he taunted me, threatening to carry one of my cats onto the farm shop roof and drop it, to test whether it would land on its feet.

And so Dirk tagged along. Within minutes we spotted Dirk's classmate, Robbie Dibbler. He was inspecting the tiny fairy garden supplies.

Apparently, some ladies liked to put together little plant pots then add in ceramic castles, frogs, fairies and stuff like that. Pretty neat. Among the supplies, a tiny white unicorn sparkled. We were just about to say "hey" to Robbie when he picked up the tiny unicorn—and Mr. Pinchly stepped up behind him.

"You going to buy that, Robbie?" Mr. Pinchly looked like a giant peering down into Robbie's little red face. Nervously, Robbie grabbed the bottom of his grubby t-shirt, a frayed hole in his jeans peeking out below. Mr. Pinchly shifted on his feet, still staring.

"Well? You buyin' it?" said Pinchly, nodding toward the unicorn.

"Ummm. Prolly n-n-not," Robbie said, looking at his shoes and kicking the outdoor shop's grassy floor.

"Ok. Well. No touching," Pinchly snapped. Then he was gone.

The author, left, (circa 1971) shows an early love for agriculture, helping her father and brother harvest sweet corn.

What about your family and your life do you really love?

1. ______________________________
2. ______________________________
3. ______________________________

Be thankful for these gifts
every single day!

The author, with her little brother, explores the bounds of her creativity, circa 1977.

What do you like to do that is creative—

coming straight from your experiences

and your imagination?

Draw a picture of it here!

Ms. Wargel and her brothers find simple fun on the farm in the mid-70s.

Who do you find fun with?

What makes them so special to you?

My Friends:

___

___

___

Why they're special:

___

___

___

___

___

___

___

___